For Thomas Morris
who was promised a book
J.R.

For Thomas, Rebecca and Pete
D.H.

Four Winds Press
Macmillan Publishing Company
866 Third Avenue
New York, NY 10022

Collier Macmillan Canada, Inc.
1200 Eglinton Avenue East
Suite 200
Don Mills, Ontario M3C 3N1

First published 1991 in Great Britain by J M
Dent & Sons Ltd, London
First American edition 1991

Printed in Italy
1 2 3 4 5 6 7 8 9 10

Richardson, Jean.
Thomas's sitter   by Jean Richardson.
p.   cm.
Summary: Thomas resists his mother's attempts
to find the perfect babysitter for him and his
baby sister Katy Victoria, until he encounters
the inventive Dan and his fun-filled activities.
ISBN 0-02-776146-0
[1. Babysitters–Fiction.] I. Title
PZ7.R39485Th 1991
[E]–dc20
90–13799 CIP AC

Thomas's Sitter

Jean Richardson

ILLUSTRATED BY
Dawn Holmes

Four Winds Press
New York

Katy Victoria lay in her crib making funny little noises, and everyone thought she was wonderful—except Thomas!

Thomas was disappointed. He'd imagined that a new brother or sister would be fun. Someone he could play with. Someone who could run (but not as fast as he could). Someone who could climb (but not as high as he could).

Katy Victoria needed lots of looking after and wanted to be cuddled whenever she cried.

It seemed to Thomas that she *always* cried when he wanted to show his mother his latest painting, or tell his father what he had done at school.

One day Thomas's mother said she had something to tell him. He sat on her lap and hugged her tight.

"Tom," she said, smiling as he tickled her cheek with his eyelashes. "I'm going back to work soon, so we'll have to find someone to look after you and Katy Victoria. We're going to get a babysitter."

Thomas was furious.

When his mother had been at work before, he'd always gone home with his friend Matthew. They'd had races in the garden, Thomas on his tricycle and Matthew driving his red car.

Sometimes Matthew's mother would pop them both in the bath and later read them a story. Once Thomas had stayed the night at Matthew's.

Now, thanks to Katy Victoria, he would have to come home from school with a *babysitter*.

Whenever his parents mentioned the word *babysitter*, Thomas ran away with his fingers in his ears.

But he wondered what she would be like. Would she be old, like his grandma? Would she be strict, like his teacher? Would she like Katy Victoria best?

Lots of babysitters came to meet Thomas and Katy Victoria, and Thomas was as naughty as he could be.

All the babysitters loved Katy Victoria, but none of them wanted to cope with Thomas.

One afternoon when he was playing in his sandbox, Thomas heard his mother calling him.

He got up slowly. He suspected that it was yet another babysitter. How could he get rid of this one?

He scooped up a bucket of sand and tipped it over his head. He had sand in his ears, sand down his neck, sand in his shorts, and sand in his shoes. He even smeared some over his face. Then Thomas went indoors.

He found his mother talking to a young man with the wildest hair he'd ever seen. It stood out around his face in a halo of tight curls.

Thomas stared up at him in surprise. Whoever was this?

"Dan, this is Tom, my rebel sandboy," his mother said.

"Tom, meet Dan, artist, handyman, gardener, and perhaps your babysitter."

Dan came right out into the garden and helped Thomas build a big sand castle.

He promised to show him how to make paper airplanes that really flew, to play soccer with him, to set up a swing, to . . .

Dan promised to do so many exciting things that Thomas felt it sounded almost too good to be true.

"A real swing?" he said.

"And can Matthew play on it?"

"No problem," said Dan.

From then on Dan came to look after Thomas and Katy Victoria every day except Saturday and Sunday.

He arrived on his bike. One day he gave Thomas a ride on it, though his legs weren't long enough to reach the pedals.

Dan waited outside school with Katy Victoria in her stroller for Thomas to come out. Thomas could spot his hair at once, and when the sun glinted on it, it seemed to be on fire. Thomas was very proud of Dan.

Sometimes they all went to the park. Dan always remembered to bring some stale bread so that they could feed the ducks.

Sometimes Matthew came home with them, and Thomas let him have a turn on the swing Dan had made.

Dan showed the boys how to make a tent, and he barbecued hot dogs for them.

"Can I have a babysitter?" Matthew asked when his mother came to collect him.

When they played battleships in the bath, Dan didn't mind how much Thomas splashed him.

One thing puzzled Thomas, and at last he asked Dan about it. "Are you a real babysitter? You don't look like one."

Dan looked up from bathing Katy Victoria.

"I like taking care of things and people," he said. "I guess I'm a babysitter and I'm also a Thomas-sitter. Does that answer your question?"

Thomas thought it did.

Thomas told his mother about Dan being a Thomas-sitter, and how he was miles better than any babysitter.

"I'm glad you like him," she said. "We spent ages trying to find the right person for you."

"But I thought you got him for Katy Victoria," said Thomas, remembering how his sister had always seemed to come first.

"Ye–es. But almost anyone could look after Katy Victoria. She just needs someone who understands babies. It was much harder to find someone who would understand a Thomas as well."

That night in bed, Thomas thought about what his mother had said.
Thomas's sitter was someone specially chosen for him. Though
to be fair, they wouldn't have needed Dan without Katy Victoria.

So baby sisters weren't so bad, he decided. And after all, *one* day she would be able to run (though not as fast as he could) . . . and climb (though not as high as he could)!